'The author is a comparative newcomer to children's books; on this evidence, he should go far.'
The Independent on Sunday

'A handsome creation.'
The Children's Bookseller

'Perfect for newly developing readers and great to share.'
Primary Times

'Watch out for this new kid on the children's books block, you will be won over!'
Librarymice.com

'I loved everything about this book.'
Bookbag

For
Thomas and Euan,
my rootin'-tootin' nephews!

Text and illustrations copyright © 2012 Alex T. Smith
First published in Great Britain in 2012 by Hodder Children's Books

The right of Alex T. Smith to be identified as the Author and Illustrator of this
Work has been asserted by him in accordance with the Copyright, Designs and
Patents Act 1988.

FIRST EDITION

10 9 8 7 6 5 4 3 2

A catalogue record for this book is available from the British Library

978 1 444 90928 9

Printed in China

The paper and board used in this paperback by Hodder Children's Books
are natural recyclable products made from wood grown in sustainable forests.
The manufacturing processes conform to the environmental regulations of
the country of origin.

Hodder Children's Books
a division of Hachette Children's Books
338 Euston Road, London NW1 3BH
www.hachette.co.uk

CLAUDE

in the Country

ALEX T. SMITH

Have you met Claude?
Here he is now.
Hello, Claude!

Beret

Claude $\longrightarrow$

Dashing jumper

Claude is a dog.

Claude is a small dog.

Claude is a small, plump dog who wears
a beret and a very dashing jumper.

He lives in a house with his owners,
Mr and Mrs Shinyshoes...

...and his best friend, Sir Bobblysock.

Sir Bobblysock is both a sock
and quite bobbly.

When Mr and Mrs Shinyshoes dash out the door to work each morning, Claude whips out his beret from under his pillow, and decides what adventure to go on.

Where will Claude and Sir Bobblysock go today?

It was Thursday morning and the day before had been a Wednesday. A wet Wednesday. Because their raincoats were still at the dry cleaners, Claude and Sir Bobblysock hadn't been able to go on an adventure. They had had to stay indoors.

Sir Bobblysock had busied himself writing his life story and Claude had busied himself being bored.

sigh...

First, he had thrown himself down on the carpet and pretended to be poorly until Sir Bobblysock looked at him and gave him some attention.

When this didn't work, Claude did some running around in circles, watched a very interesting film about cowboys, and then he gave a concert for all his other friends. It had been a rip-roaring success.

CLANG! CLANG! CLANG!

Mr Smelly Sock

Dr. Chewed Squeakybone

Dame Nibbled-Slipper

←Keith

But now it was Thursday and
the sun was out. Claude needed
some fresh air.

'I think I will go to the countryside,'
he said. So that's what he did.

Sir Bobblysock decided to go too, as he was stuck on a tricky chapter of his book and a day out would do him some good. He was a little worried about the countryside, as he had heard that it was very green and he often found that green took the colour out of his face.

But he decided to be brave and the two friends bustled off.

It didn't take them long to find the countryside. Claude was surprised by how very big it was and how very green. Sir Bobblysock decided that he rather liked it too, after all.

The Countryside

19

There was plenty to see.

Claude looked at the grass.

Claude looked at the flowers.

And a rather startled rabbit
looked at Claude!

Before very long, Claude smelt a rather peculiar smell. Whilst it wasn't a horrible smell, it certainly was rather whiffy. It smelt like mud and a little like Sir Bobblysock, when he had been a bit grumpy and not washed for a week.

WELCOME TO
WOOLLYBOTTOM FARM

Claude soon discovered
that the smell was coming
from a farm.

23

He had never been to a farm before, so he decided to go and see what it was all about. Sir Bobblysock popped a peg on his nose and hopped along behind.

Claude hadn't got very far when a very jolly woman in some dungarees and wellington boots saw him and started waving.

He quickly combed his ears
and Sir Bobblysock adjusted
his bobbles.

'Hello!' cried the woman, marching over to them. 'My name is Mrs Cowpat and I am the farmer here!'

'Hello,' said Claude, shaking her hand with his paw. 'My name is Claude and this is my friend, Sir Bobblysock. Can we help you be a farmer for the day?'

COUNTRY FAIR
at
WOOLLYBOTTOM FARM
starts at 3pm
CAKE STALLS!
COMPETITIONS!
FUNNY SHAPED VEGETABLES!

27

Mrs Cowpat said 'yes, of course,' and that she would be jolly glad of the help as she had a very busy day ahead of her. It turned out that today was the day of the County Fair, when people from all over the place gathered together in the countryside to parade their nice animals about and show each other their funny-shaped vegetables.

Sir Bobblysock liked the sound of that and so did Claude.

28

'The County Fair takes place in one
of my fields this afternoon,'
explained Mrs Cowpat.
'You two can help me get
everything ready!'

She handed Claude
a pair of wellies and
they all set off.

29

Because of all the rain the day before, there were lots of muddy puddles on the farm.

Sir Bobblysock, who on the whole didn't really like anything grubby, carefully hopped around them and was pleased that he hadn't got his bobbles in a mess.

Claude made sure that he splashed and sploshed in every single one of them.

Some puddles were deeper than
they seemed...

32

The first job was to feed all the chickens and collect the eggs. Claude liked chickens. He liked the way their bottoms wobbled as they walked.

As Claude searched all over the chicken coop for the eggs, he practised walking like a chicken. Wobble! Wobble! Wobble! went his bottom and he found that, although he enjoyed it, bottom wobbling was rather tiring.

It made Sir Bobblysock
feel a bit giddy just watching him.

35

Claude was very good at finding the eggs. He had soon gathered a whole basketful and even found an egg hiding under his beret!

'The next very important thing I need to do,' said Mrs Cowpat, 'is to round up all of my sheep. Usually, I let them go and play in my fields, but today I need to gather them up so they don't make a nuisance of themselves during the County Fair.'

Claude and Sir Bobblysock listened very carefully to the farmer as she explained that she had a special dog called a sheepdog that did all the rounding up for her.

'I blow my whistle,' explained Mrs Cowpat, 'and do a bit of pointing and shouting, and my dog dashes about the field, gathers all the sheep into a group and brings them into their barn.'

It turned out, however, that Mrs Cowpat's dog was currently on holiday, so she asked if Claude would do the job for her.

Claude agreed. Sir Bobblysock sat out on account of his stiff knee.

39

Claude had never been a sheepdog before. But he found he was rather good at it.

He popped his beret under his jumper, put on his sweatband and jogged all over the fields shouting 'HELLO!' and waving to all the sheep.

Unfortunately this didn't
round them up. They just
stood and stared at him, wondering
what on earth was going on.

41

Claude decided to try a different approach.

He jogged up to the sheep who looked like she was in charge and asked most politely if she wouldn't mind going into the barn for the afternoon.

The sheep blushed at being asked so nicely. Then she whistled to her friends and they all trooped into the barn.

'Well done, Claude!' said Mrs Cowpat when he jogged back to her. 'You make a wonderful sheepdog!'

Sir Bobblysock beamed with pride.

43

The next job was the horses. Claude was very excited to see these. All the cowboys in the film he'd watched the day before had ridden horses and looked very smart doing so, too.

'These horses need a bit of exercise,' explained Mrs Cowpat. 'Would you like to take them for a ride?'

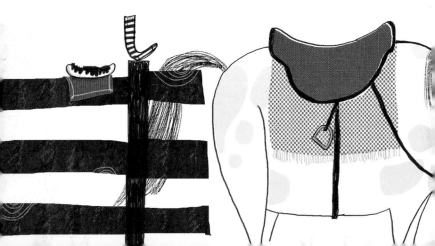

Claude nodded excitedly, but
Sir Bobblysock declined politely.
He'd ridden a horse before and it
hadn't ended well, so he decided
to sit on the fence and have a
chocolate eclair instead.

At first, Claude enjoyed his horse ride and felt just like a cowboy. He even found a lasso in his beret, which he waggled above his head enthusiastically.

Then, unfortunately, the horse got a bit carried away and Claude didn't enjoy the ride half as much...

Mrs Cowpat quickly untangled Claude and helped him smooth down his ears, which had got rather windswept in all the excitement.

'I think we could all do with a nice cup of tea and a sit down,' said Mrs Cowpat. The three farmers shared a flask of tea and had a slice of fruitcake each.

It was lovely to have a rest for a few minutes and Claude and Sir Bobblysock were just closing their eyes for a moment when…

The biggest cockerel you have ever
seen crowed in Claude's ear.

It frightened the life out of him and Sir Bobblysock was a nervous wreck – he'd never been one for sudden loud noises. A grasshopper had leapt out at him once and he had to take to his bed for three days with his eye mask on, and a Relaxing Sounds of the Rainforest record playing in the background.

Claude didn't want all of that to
happen again, so before the
cockerel could make another noise,
Claude threw a big piece of cake
into its mouth and popped a pair of
earmuffs on Sir Bobblysock.

'Let's do something else now,' said
Mrs Cowpat. 'Something a bit
calmer perhaps...'

And she showed Claude and
Sir Bobblysock her haystacks,
her cows, her fearsome-looking
bull and, lastly, her pigs.

54

Claude sniffed a big sniffy sniff. 'Aha!' he thought. It was the pigs that smelt a little bit like cheesy socks! And he couldn't help noticing that they were covered in mud and looked an awful mess.

Mrs Cowpat suddenly looked at her watch and gasped.

'Oh, my goodness!' she cried. 'The County Fair is about to begin and I haven't got everything ready. These pigs are competing in the Most Beautiful Pigs competition and look at the state of them! Would you mind giving them a quick wash whilst I go and check that all the stalls have been set up properly?'

Claude nodded and helped Mrs
Cowpat pull out a long hose and an
old tin bath.

'Thank you,' she said, dashing off.
'I'll come back in a few minutes and
see how you are getting on.'

Claude looked at the mucky pigs.
Then he looked at the old tin bath.
Then he looked at Sir Bobblysock
and Sir Bobblysock looked back at
Claude.

Then Claude popped his beret
under his jumper, tied his ears
above his head, pushed his sleeves
up and set to work.

When Mrs Cowpat came back she wasn't at all expecting to see what she saw...

'Oh!' said Mrs Cowpat.
'They look...err...lovely...'

But she couldn't say any more, as the clock struck three o'clock and the County Fair had begun.

There was such a lot to see.
And an awful lot to do.

They sampled the cakes at the
cake stall (just in time for their
three o'clock snack).

62

They looked on in amazement whilst somebody showed off her prize pumpkins.

They clapped loudly when a man won a prize for his cucumber.

And they held their breath as a very
snooty-looking man with a
clipboard marched around Mrs
Cowpat's pigs, judging them in the
Most Beautiful Pigs competition.

Eventually, he scribbled something on his pad and announced that Mrs Cowpat had won! Claude threw his beret up in the air with excitement.

The snooty judge rolled his eyes and marched off across the field to judge the Most Cross-looking Bull competition.

Claude and Sir Bobblysock carried on looking round. There was a Most Handsome Dog competition in ten minutes' time, and Claude was just deciding whether to enter when from across the field there came the most dreadful noise.

RGGGGHHHH!

Claude and Sir Bobblysock dashed to where the noise was coming from. It didn't take them long to discover what was going on.

The snooty-looking judge had obviously done something to make one of the big bulls very angry and it was now chasing him around the enclosure. Its big spiky horns were heading straight for the judge's bottom!

'Somebody save him!' cried
Mrs Cowpat, looking very worried.
Nobody knew what to do.

71

Just then Claude had an idea.
He remembered the cowboy film
he had watched the day before.
Bravely, Claude pulled his lasso out
from under his beret and strutted
into the ring.

Sir Bobblysock's bobbles shook
with fright and he didn't dare look,
except he couldn't help peeping.

The angry bull was galumphing about like a lunatic and the poor judge was running as fast as he could to keep out of the way.

'Help,' he shouted.

Claude stood in the middle of the ring and whirled his lasso about above his head.

He whirled it and twirled it and twirled it and whirled it.

The judge was still galloping around the ring with the bull right on his heels. Suddenly, the judge's shoes slipped on the slippery grass and whooooooooosh...

…he skidded across the enclosure
and landed SPLAT face first in a
cowpat!

The bull screeched to a halt.
Then, with steam coming from its
nostrils, it started to scrape its hoofs
on the ground. Scrape! Scrape!
Scrape! Then – KABOOM
off it went like a bomb.

It ran at full speed, with its head tucked down and its horns glinting in the sunshine.
It was just inches from the judge's bottom, when Claude flung his lasso up into the air.

Everything was silent.

Sir Bobblysock could hear his heart
thumping in his head.

Claude took a sharp intake of breath
and then...

...when the moment was just right,
he flicked his paw and the lasso
tightened around one of the bull's
horns. He had captured it!

Claude then pulled and pulled with all his might and, eventually, the bull came to a stop.

He walked up to it with a very determined little walk.

'Now,' he said, 'you are being a very naughty boy!' And he waggled a finger at the bull. 'Are you going to stop chasing this nice man?'

The bull nodded.

'Good,' said Claude, and he reached under his beret and found a cupcake he'd stashed there for emergencies. He gave it to the bull, who nibbled away at it politely.

The crowd that had gathered roared with applause and the judge shook Claude's paw and said, 'thank you'. He didn't seem that snooty any more!

Mrs Cowpat came running over to Claude, with Sir Bobblysock hopping behind her.

'What a brave dog you are!' she said breathlessly. 'I don't suppose you'd like to come and be a farmer here on my farm would you? You'd be super!'

Claude thought about it for a minute. He had had a lovely time – and all the fresh air had certainly put some colour in his and Sir Bobblysock's cheeks – but he did like his cosy bed at Mr and Mrs Shinyshoes' house.

He looked at Sir Bobblysock and
could see that all that bull business
had been a bit too much for him.
He looked like he needed one of his
long lie-downs in a darkened room.
He politely explained all of this to
Mrs Cowpat.

She was a bit disappointed but said
that she understood. 'You must
come back and visit soon,' she said.

Then she gave Claude and Sir
Bobblysock a lift home in her
tractor.

When Mr and Mrs Shinyshoes came home a bit later, Claude and Sir Bobblysock were tucked up in bed.

'Good gracious!' said Mrs Shinyshoes, wafting her hand about. 'There's a frightful whiff in here! Do you think it's Claude?'

Mr Shinyshoes laughed. 'I don't know,' he said. 'Let's ask him when he wakes up. We can also ask him where on earth this lasso has come from!'

In his bed Claude smiled a little smile.

Of course he knew were it had come from.

And we do too, don't we?

Interesting things to look
for in the countryside:

Cowpats

Beautiful pigs

Grumpy bulls
(BEWARE!)

Wobbly bottomed
chickens

Don't forget to take
your wellies!

And remember to keep
your eye out for Claude and
Sir Bobblysock – you never know
where they might pop up next.